QUILTED

GEORGIA-MAE TAN

BAILBROOK LANE

First published 2024. Published in the United Kingdom
Tan, Georgia-mae
Quilted / Georgia-mae Tan.

Cover design and illustrations by Georgia-mae Tan

eBook ISBN 978-1-913557-06-5
Paperback ISBN 978-1-913557-07-2

Bailbrook Lane is an imprint of Xelium Ltd.

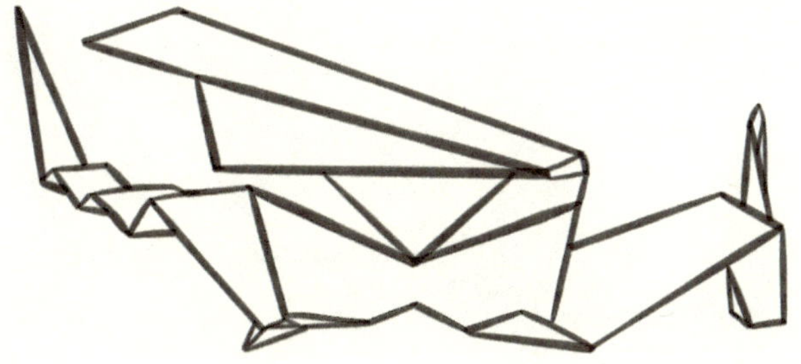

Contents

Leucanthemum vulgare
Oxeye daisy

paddling pools

a baby birthed from the sun
with pink leaves
printed on the back of her neck
up against a blue sky

you do not know how arms will reach
to hold you in the neon light
circling + unbinding
travelling in a paradox of apprehension and ease
skin peals down the sides of your thumbs
corralled effigies will hold the bones before you

swimming in golden seas,
surrounded by milk flowers that
nod under fingers
and weave solace in the cradle.

dear god!

god exists in the library
I know this much to be true: I saw it
between ordered rows of A-Z
travel guides, philosophy, religious experiences
are the girls who pray with freshly painted nails
letting christ into their life - .....lord give us strength.....
who don't know their boyfriends grieve in some sad
masochistic way
whilst they laugh about the 'patriarchal paradigm'
in miniskirts and hair extensions
forgive me father for I have sinned
filing down acrylics, buckling five inch heals
with trembling double ironies
liberated from the fragile shackles of monogamy
but tied to etchings between walls L + J (love forever)
they perch round the table in a seance of ohmygods
light falling, casting half-moons on blood red polish
strong enough to dig up the dead
to wake to the outside world with their bodies inverted
hand in heart, heart in hand
freshly manicured - *let us pray*.
they do not go quietly announcing their amens
as they call upon the father, son and the holy ghost.

self-serving or the end of an infomercial

Please take your seat _______ will be your server today
Sir, your food will arrive in just two seconds, thank you, yes
Sir, I heard you the first time.
Sir, please sit down
Sir, I apologise we cannot -
Sir, that was incredibly rude, I will have to report that
Sir, please do not touch me, sit down, your meal will come
to you
Sir, I am going to have to ask you take your seat.
Sir, please sit down
Sir, sir- please, if I may... yes
Sir, your meal will come to you.
Sir, I am going to have to call my manager.
Sir, I am going to have to call security.
I'm going to have to...Thomas can you-
Sir, please
look
Sir, hello, what seems to be the problem?
Sir, yes sir- we will sort it in just a second. No need to-
Sir, Sit Down or you will be escorted off the premises
You will be escorted off the premises.
Do not touch the waitresses.
Excuse me?
If I may ask you to take your seat
Sir, I will be with you in just two moments.
Sir, this is not funny - we have a no-
I'm calling security.

ERROR: eat up!

Sir,
Do not pass go,
Do not collect £200.

premonitions

I do not know how to smile with my teeth
baby   teeth
that crushed butterflies' wings

the trees nod in disagreement
spools of sunshine ginkgo
that litters the pavement.

next summer
frogs will face the Lily-pads   bent back
cracked on the axiom   moon-bitten

whilst autumn's dried persimmon leaves &
the   lopped   choy sum heart
will make me fall under the brief intimacy of childhood again

of chopped hair buried deep in pillowcases
+ primary colours laid out in blocks
of dancing on single slats of sun-dried wood
+ jumping waves in dead blue winter

If this is not created
do we dare dream the infinite
Truthfully then
                i am unborn

& i would take back the daisies breaking
Beneath heals two sizes too big
strawberry gum stuck to the soles

Sellotape the pages that illustrate the sea
Press heart shaped thumbs to a kingfisher's breast
And breathe out the sweet scent of jibing derision
That gnaws at my bones, past silver birch trees, eating through
ghosts.

Galanthus nivalis
Snowdrop

the last time i saw you at the train station on the 20th june, *4.47pm*

{keep your eyes on the prize my wild child}

god you stand with such / confidence cutting / echoes with the / heavy weight of your shoulders / they droop like anything / always late / you (i) turn back / i wait / s can't decide which train to get / i see you / i want to ask you if you are going to / the party on sunday / *are you ok how are you* / your brow knits that brown trench coat / i want to ask you how london is *will be* / we never did plan it / you didn't know / i want to cry / i want to run to my mother / i want to run to your mother / i want to ask her where her son went / i want to ask her if she knows / i want to sit and sip black tea with your mother and my mother conversing over (largely) inconsequential matters / like the current micro economical state of south africa / and how your brother was named after a saint / as we obey the ritual in slow gentile customs / unknowing / i wonder if you still sleep outside the house / if italy would have ever worked / you always said you wanted to go / it is june after all / and the seashells you / slipped into my pockets / are on my windowsill / i want your shoulder / on my shoulder / against the back of an elephant / tangible like the bark of an ancient tree / that would hide the hole you showed me in your stomach / because it ~~did not~~ never did beat out of your (my) chest / perhaps not yet / that small heart of pink tenderness / sinews and muscle / you walk you, do not see me / chupa chup (~~my~~ the best) / cool cat / the weight does not lift / the moon eclipses the star but / you are kind / and i cannot swallow / the sunflower still sits on my shelf / bloomsday plays carefully / in the back of my pocket / oh see how you grow. //

paper houses

ah kong, lu chiak pah ah buay
you can't go anywhere on an empty stomach
least not where lightning strikes the roofs of temples
i wonder if he's eaten

i walk down the slope and think of how it looks
like a scene from a more nuanced kung fu panda
but the oranges are stacked high and the bats
still cling to the beam - babies onto mothers,
onto fathers, onto red wood
he would have cut and painted it himself
with h and c dancing on the sun-dried slats
despite colourful expletives echoed through tinned roofs
when wood hit the floor and mo hid under the table.

the casket lay in the middle of the living room
doors remained open through the night, for visiting
mirrors clothed in white muslin,
so he wouldn't be able to see his missing reflection
stuffed with tufts of cotton wool
coins are heavy on the eyes.

ingot edges opened - a subtler origami
hell's currency dictated by the living
ah mah had collected them in fat plastic bags
and we sat on stools, dipping in the joss paper,
we burned a paper house, 12 feet tall and 8 feet wide,
blue like the mansion on leith street
we burned all the things you wanted and all those you did not
have.

i closed the circle to nurture the shock of the impact
7 times round 3 knelt and 4 across the bridge
dropping 5 cents into the water to send you over
next time, i'll have a personal word with the ferryman.

sometimes i dream in another language
to dare even to remember the bones picked with
chopsticks and placed so delicately in the porcelain urn
the yellow ribbon cut and pinned; knees hollowed with
indents.

but i fall
we walk in order twice round the house then
once through the middle washing our hands and feet

i climb over the balcony and into the sunken bowl of water
i step out onto sun burned grass
and as told, breathe in luck for your soft rest.

on early spring

i

you wanted to see down the funicular and imitate parallel lines,
to articulate carefully crafted fifths
that you forgot any constant rooted within you. peeling layers -
a longing to feel soft peach skin revealing knots like kneaded
dough rising at the break
only to revel in the constancy and bloom.

ii

fall through the stagnant water that, which glitters green, but
only when the shallow blurs, blows to buff. you will be born,
small in the noble curve of a winter's dew drop those which
change to quiet bluebells in spring. promise
because we have not matured enough
to sit on the precipice of wanting and self-generating

iii

a balance on shaky wheels, we turn to movement which
reflects inside us
the yolks' petals that drip down foreheads at night breaking
gold
because O wouldn't pearls be a chore! there is some delicacy in
this i'll admit.

iv

yet, when we return, we find
we are too small to stake claim on the obdurating retinal glow
of the soft, almost laughable clock-hands when the morning
light cuts the table, bending eyes through glass you turn to face
the little sun.

First impressions

...You said that you might get me socks for my birthday?

it could be, but if you kept telling me it was socks, I probably
would expect it to change - due to *you telling me.*

HOWEVER

If you were telling me and *I had anticipated that, I would not be
led to believe you* and it would turn out to be socks anyhow,
then I would now think you were getting me socks and not be
surprised when you do.

HOWEVER

I could anticipate that I'd anticipated, I would then think you
'weren't' getting me socks but of course, then you are and
therefore would not think I was getting socks and
be *pleasantly surprised when it turned out to be true.*

HOWEVER

I could anticipate that I'd anticipate my anticipation, that is *I
would think that it wouldn't be socks but in thinking it isn't, I would
then inadvertently be thinking it is..* (in me thinking it is not socks
I would be realising that it rather was socks as I had obviously
pre-guessed). Then my guessing that my initial guess was in
fact the guess which was my secondary guess, superseded by
the tertiary guess of the secondary guess overruling it, leads
eventually to, the quaternary guess, which it is, the correct
conclusion to come to – *the fact that you are <u>indeed</u> getting me socks
for my birthday.*

Campanula rotundifolia
Bellflower

now cracks a noble heart[*]

there is no present satisfaction   not yet
for to see the mind would defeat the purpose entirely.
colours unknown. by the collar of your church.
sparks a genome habitat for wild dancing.
[that bacchic frenzy].   one   that
two that
we might   act
conjure the tangible to see. ourselves
etched   in another life. where
laces are strawberry. butter, cold. meat, charred.
half circadian, to the cicada under a midwestern sky.
only welt when she heard you cry.
blue wings. you are forgiven.
I will not let you fall into your own hands,
but promise me to only catch the sun when it does not lie
counter clock come back
you spur
at first flight. a cockatoo folded in tea leaves and yet, the
bespectacled kingfisher watches on.

---

[*] 'Now cracks a noble heart' Horatio's last words to his best friend in Shake-
speare's eponymous Hamlet (5.2. 397-98).

oracle's whispers (crown violets)
first published by FlowerMouth Press

The axle wings unbroken,
as glitter cut my mother's hands.

cresting/moulting
   first published in the Foyle Young Poets Anthology 2023

my teeth fell out of the tree
mango stained, smiling
i strung them up on a washing line
pearls of puckered rice

sewn by those on bended knee
sat on upturned buckets, laughing
when frowns morph to edges, while
their grandmothers hold the lychee seeds
that mine buries in her hands

just as she mourned her son
when gold was etched upon her forehead
cheeks now droop like curved grapes
(they rid the sighs,
                whilst the burnt embers billow.)

she holds me like a baby

binding the legs tucked beneath,
olive meat and splayed toes
with wide almond eyes which carry vices
by morning, amidst half moons

Now I lay limbic stretched against the light
As a whirlpool gathers beneath my feet
glowing + pinned sure

time will always blur those under me
washed up records of recognition

unfolding in a brief notion of ease
and i grow to moult the thorny things.

Outside Ealing station

the trees breathe through light
as feet pad on glacial concrete.
moon, you sit so silently
stitched under purple hues
(blue and red) refracted through lenses.
clementine compels the retinal glow
you speak for autumn, free from spring
after the sun-stained jasmine pearls
sealed in all the creatures of our mythology.

Epicurean

I wish I could tell you about the three dead girls down by
the lake
arabella, alexandra, antonia
or maybe anastasia and allegra.
those tiny prom queens who sing songs of jealously and longing
fingers wretched against the sunlight
- like an off-brand Tim Burton film
but with the distant sound of trains in the background.

Starlets floating like balloons in lose leaf tea,
Before sinking their childish naivety in linen floral singlets
and blood oranges that line mahogany tables.
Most trapped under blue-stained glass windows bending light
Lockets that hold safe-keeping, cut for
your modern-day amethysts
An artefact to be held true, preserved
like fish bones collected in the market.

They fill the sweet-loving of
pressed chrysanthemums in pockets
That seal an eternal hemlock dance
concealed by the long hem of calico skirts

All but a spectral flicker in the corner of my eye
The shadow moves in the bathtub, bent back by
The cream curtain.
Mother, I was ill for two weeks straight and
I think I saw the inside of a madhouse.

Actias luna
Luna moth

Growing pains

moon etched   swabbed in   cardamon patchwork

we fall   into   the brief shadows   held at the root

some   palpable joy   shatters the hydrangea

shakes the seeds   between the bushes   when the spit

pools on my   belly   I cradle the   cracked   sea shells

which smooth   the   edges   a   sheltering   cry

we are all somebody's baby   yawning

through   growing pains

like   a   mishima novel but i don't   have the

hands or legs

to   feed it.

I do not   bear the brunt   of it to

be a   guilty apologist

opulent and adorned with gems   those   fragile hearts
that

                            equate

this sentiment   to some sort   of clarity

on   sunday   you smell like   ravioli   & scoured dish soap

I wonder   what would do   to   allow the rain to   pass

through us   when you hold   the bones   of a dying   swallow

baked under   the   hot sun   before

you   close and

we   bury it   in

the   heart

of   a   sandcastle.

Advertisements to the moon

I believe in the natural state of the cosmos/ a return to an entropic order/ a pull across the border line which reserves/ running through a cemetery on New Year's Eve/ or skipping lunch on a <u>Tuesday afternoon</u>/ for you/ Because if I started to question/ my eyes would see and my heart would beat without it.

There is no end to life which has already begun/ The wail of the summer crickets marks the dawn/ for girls made of stardust/ the ones Venus comforts at night/wrapping arms around their slender bodies/come, my sweetpea, tonight you dance with the stars.

The vegetable-hearted/girls with broken streaks painted across their backs/the ones blackbirds court like junebugs/who laugh with hysterical pleasures/wash up chipped tea cups and run through dreams/ do not cut their toenails on the midnight train/nor walk on ground uncharted.

But my darling you/you squash emperor moths beneath your feet/rage with mars in your belly/you do not need to pick blackberries/to see that your blood-stained purple/grows flowers in the grave/so breathe out the sweet scent of jibing derision/fold up the paper hearts you throw/to the Sargasso Sea/and with this you too can be ____/for only 2.99.

taroko

we stretched to see how far we could swim
before the dawn broke through and
our skin breathed sun dappled against the light.

It was then, they say Ascanius first shot in war.
The first arrow pierced,   brave lion
A swift displacement through apricot air,
The plume of smoke drawn, gilded through fetters.
Clay ground soft beneath his padded feet.
He prayed first to Jupiter, only for the trial of Mars.
Do not let him get you, Ascanius,
For even Troy is not large enough for you.
Promise the milk-white bull, but only to remember the cause.
Justice prevails yet only when it is sweetest.
When Athena lit the storeroom she saw, Telemachus, a boy.
Raging and strong. *Furor* will not overtake you now.
For along the walls of the battlefield, at the break of a new day,
flowers do grow.

As for the second Achilles,
Let no wound be hideous, nor armour falter,
Let Turnus face a death unyielding.
Prove it only by an *aristeia* bottled at the hands of the gods,
Certain and unhurried,   savage lion
Guard the boss of your shield,
Hold close your soldiers,
Cross the river which commands a fated victory.

Jade Dragon/ midnight dinner club

Perhaps I can tempt you to my favourite:
Salted fish or Chicken feet
With toasted garlic & soft split goji berries
Scarlet as the takeaway sign
Along Mayflower Road

Whose shopfront screams in sworded silver
Jade Dragon Takeaway
Where the cornflower overpowers the
Sweet and sour chicken,
& vegetable spring rolls
are served with dulled down chilli sauce.

A mother & son's aprons gently crease
As the bottom of steamed dumplings
or the soft twist in the midnight wax paper
of the White Rabbit candy sitting upon the counter top
I imagine she must walk on persimmon leaves.

At 11pm when all is still and stagnant
The blistered neon sign flickers shut in the window
and the dragon truly awakens
shedding its green skin
to reveal golden secrets

Eggs soaked for a century, in slack lime, hidden under the
counter
Plastic wrapped to mask the smell of ammonia
Peeling, stretched white & translucent
They grow grey snowflakes,
that wrap around my mother's thumb

Slowly, aunties begin to gather in the kitchen
a flurry of gossip, in a tongue of my own
I cannot decipher. They knead my cheeks
with Eucalyptus infused hands
Exchanging dishes and recipes of tradition.

you're tall now
look how you've grown

Between the shrill laughter and
soft clicks of mah-jong tiles;
a cigarette balanced on the edge
It is here I discover that: Only do we, rejoice
through the ice green worms of Chendol jelly

Or the salted egg yolk
Half-cooked and broken over rice, still warm
Masked by the thick smell of downstairs
Sesame oil on deep-fried
prawn toast

To eat at the Jade Dragon
is to know it is more than the commercialised tea
laden with tapioca pearls
(which brings in half the income)
or the boxed up, sickly stir-fried kung pao chicken

It is to taste pig's blood fresh in coconut broth
and feel the grit of the floor beneath your feet.
Let the sap from the peach tree stick to your gums,
whilst sweat rivulets in the valley of the back of your neck.
Laugh through wide-toothed smiles
and crack open the cereal-coated prawns of my father's
invention.

Echo the cries of uncles who cannot find the lotus-leafed
hearts
and Eat. For those who do not know how.

**'self-discovery' through late night shopping
(set to the theme of cowboy bebop)**

she flies down aisles
the trolley bar dents the curve of her wrist
rolling under lights like the flash of paparazzi cameras
or a doctor's waiting room...same monotony of 9 to 5...
the fever dream of a life gone by
where she marries a malibu man
who travels for work

but her kitchen still then consists of
taped fractures & freshly packed cabbages
overseeing the uniform barcodes of a skyscraper vigil
to the pink lady, of course – blushed red
2 for 1, tea set doilies or toilet seat cigarettes
Only today!!!

seasons change as the violet hawthorn
comes to cradle the coccyx
restocking on teas and digestives
she returns to the analgesic patterns:
bottles she hopes, slip under - the way kindness remedies
a t-shirt slogan, blueing: baby, i'm yours!!!

today, begins again, begins again, begins again
worn in coke can boots
arms stretched out at Extraordinary liberty
like the end of a coming-of-age movie
but where the jock realises he loves the rich girl
before he pulls his gun
before he goes home to a mother baking apple pie,
as his father builds a new desk.

where we'll stand together, before walking into the distance
amidst the phosphorescent porcelain plates and real shiny
guinea pigs
for it is only at the ~~checkpoint~~ checkout we remember
We are such small things.

this is what i know of the future

it is in our hands,   my dear
dreams   in golden   green
                cross   dance   zing
drum along   the wire.

The lunar dance   reflects in your eyes,
time falls again
as pools of light gather beneath lamp posts.
Breathe, softly now,
under an ever-forgiving moon
swaddled in moss,   to grow
                bound by birch bark bracelets
you are, you are, you are.

Ammonoidea
Ammonite

Acknowledgements

notes, acknowledgements and thanks

to you, the reader.

to my friends (long live djungelskog!) - for putting up with me, (my incessant lunar imagery) and for being willing but unwitting fodder for my many literary musings. *now cracks a noble heart* was written for O's birthday and *Outside Ealing station* just after a group trip to London in December of 2023. *Epicurean* was written after a late night conversation with J, *Advertisements to the moon* after a New Years' Party in 2022 and *taroko* after August Greenwood's wonderful song.

to my colleagues and friends at the egg theatre which has been the warmest and kindest testing bed for my writing I could wish for; and to anyone else I've harassed on open mic nights, readings and poetry slams.

Thank you!

Georgia-mae Tan is a two-time Foyles young poet and a member of the National Youth Theatre. She is inspired by the intricacies of everyday conversation and the small joys of nature and music. Tucked away in Bath, with her small but mighty yorkie Ollie, she writes best often in the early hours of the morning. A jasmine tea fiend and movie enthusiast, she is also a collector of stories, trinkets, seashells and fossils.

You can find her on Instagram @georgiamaetan and www.georgia-mae.com

For her artwork and blog @blueberrysnail and www.blueberrysnail.com

www.ingramcontent.com/pod-product-compliance
Lightning Source LLC
Chambersburg PA
CBHW061501210726
48287CB00007B/2610